WELCOME TO
PASSPORT TO READING
A beginning reader's ticket to a brand-new world!

Every book in this program is designed to build read-along and read-alone skills, level by level, through engaging and enriching stories. As the reader turns each page, he or she will become more confident with new vocabulary, sight words, and comprehension.

These PASSPORT TO READING levels will help you choose the perfect book for every reader.

READING TOGETHER
Read short words in simple sentence structures together to begin a reader's journey.

READING OUT LOUD
Encourage developing readers to sound out words in more complex stories with simple vocabulary.

READING INDEPENDENTLY
Newly independent readers gain confidence reading more complex sentences with higher word counts.

READY TO READ MORE
Readers prepare for chapter books with fewer illustrations and longer paragraphs.

This book features sight words from the educator-supported Dolch Sight Words List. This encourages the reader to recognize commonly used vocabulary words, increasing reading speed and fluency.

For more information, please visit passporttoreadingbooks.com.

Enjoy the journey!

Little, Brown and Company

Hachette Book Group
1290 Avenue of the Americas, New York, NY 10104
Visit us at lb-kids.com

Little, Brown and Company is a division of Hachette Book Group, Inc.
The Little, Brown name and logo are trademarks of Hachette Book Group, Inc.

The publisher is not responsible for websites (or their content)
that are not owned by the publisher.

First Edition: February 2017

Library of Congress Control Number: 2016949866

ISBNs: 978-0-316-31580-7 (pbk.), 978-0-316-31704-7 (ebook)

10 9 8 7 6 5 4 3 2 1

CW

Printed in the United States of America

Passport to Reading titles are leveled by independent reviewers applying the
standards developed by Irene Fountas and Gay Su Pinnell in *Matching Books to
Readers: Using Leveled Books in Guided Reading*, Heinemann, 1999.

Written by Magnolia Belle

LITTLE, BROWN AND COMPANY
New York   Boston

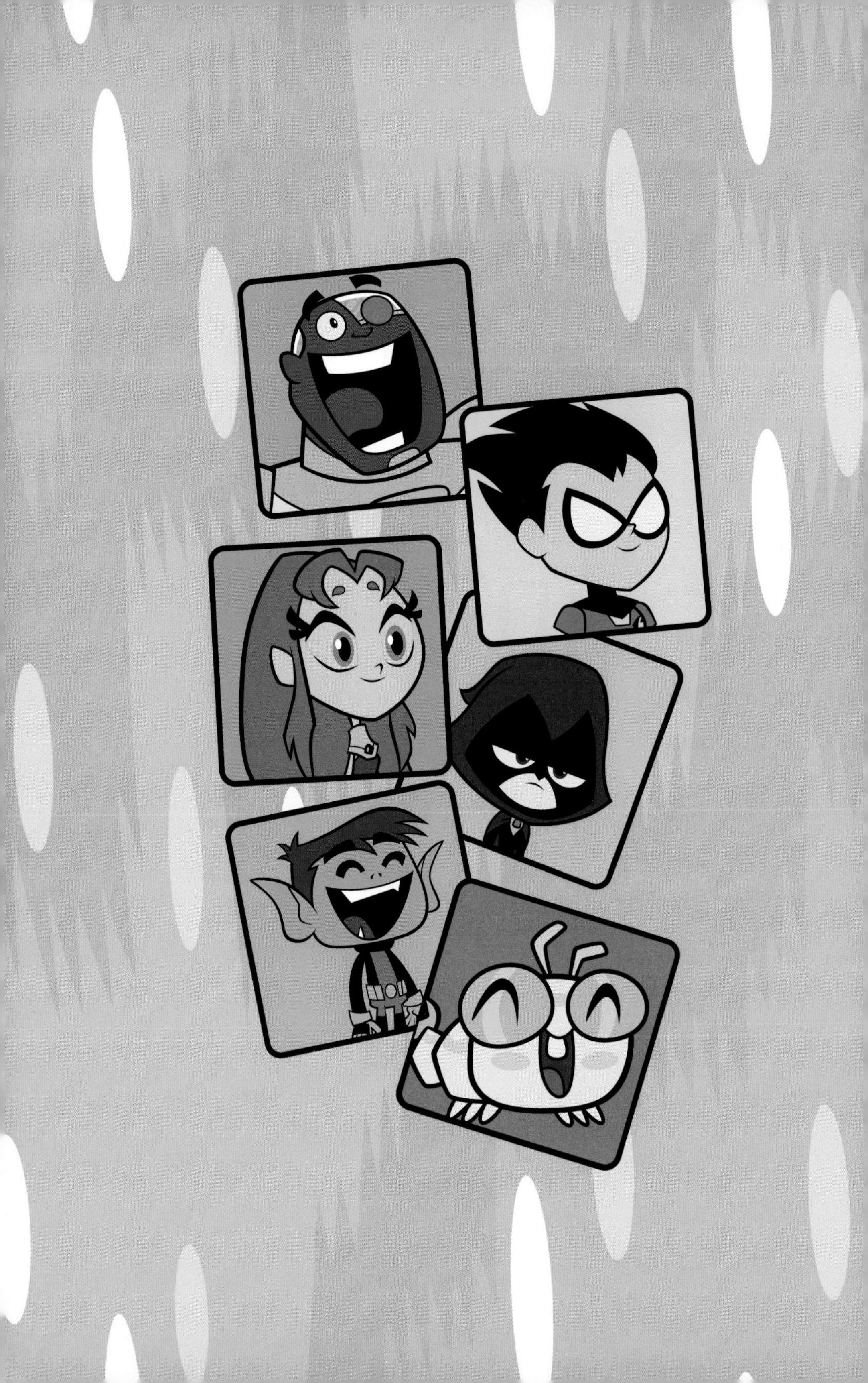

Attention, Teen Titans fans!
Look for these words when you read
this book. Can you spot them all?

berries

swimming

robot

sword

Silkie is the quiet, little pet
of the Teen Titans.

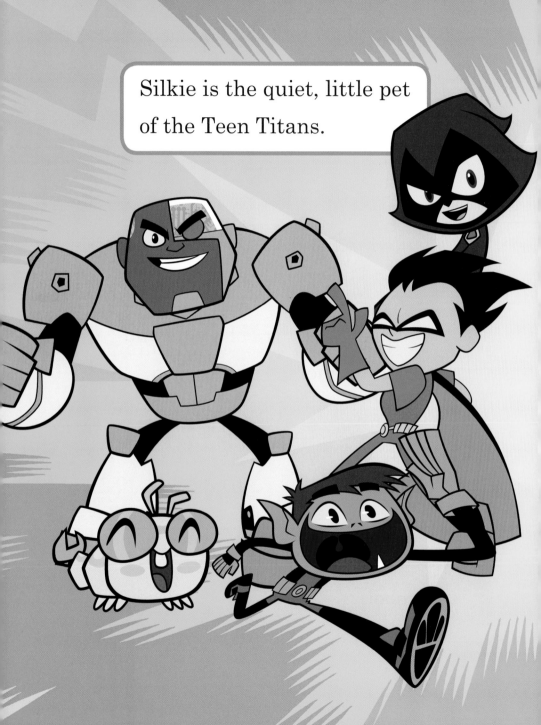

Starfire takes care of Silkie and loves him more than anything.

Silkie loves Starfire a lot, too!

Silkie likes it when Starfire gives him baths and cleans behind his ears.

He also loves it when Starfire
tickles his tummy.
It makes him happy.

Starfire calls Silkie
her little baby.

Silkie's favorite food comes in a can.

If he gets really hungry,
he will eat almost anything.
But Silkie does not like tofu!

If Silkie eats berries
from Starfire's home planet,
he grows as big as a house!

Silkie wishes he could grow wings and fly.

He is also very good at avoiding danger!

Raven likes to play dress-up with Silkie.
She calls him Princess Silkie Soft.

Silkie also likes to play dress-up with Starfire.

Silkie loves it when Cyborg reads to him...

...and when Beast Boy takes him swimming.

Beast Boy also likes
to make himself look
like Silkie!

One time, magic turned Silkie into a genius.

While Silkie was a genius, he built a giant robot.

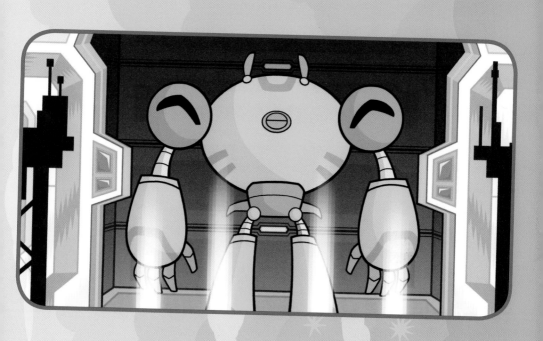

Silkie and his robot saved the world from a huge asteroid!

When Starfire goes on vacation,
she asks the other Titans
to babysit Silkie.

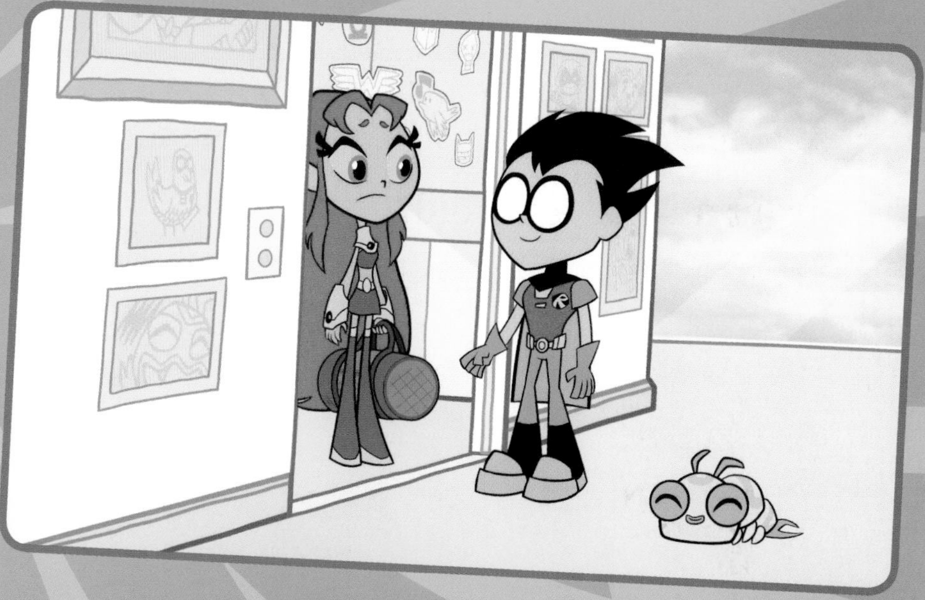

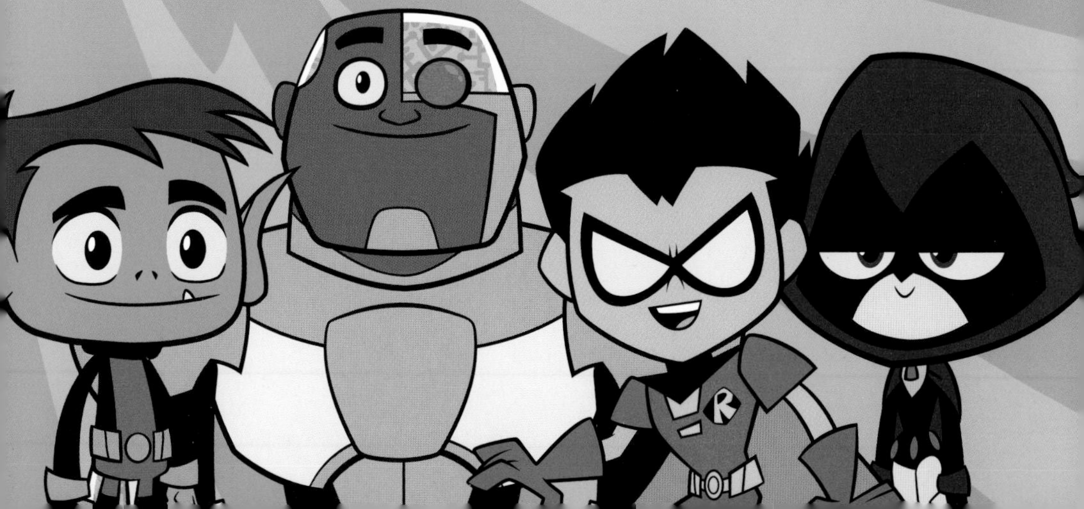

The Titans lose Silkie and have to look all over for him.

When Silkie gets lost,
he goes on many adventures.
Sophia is Silkie's new friend!

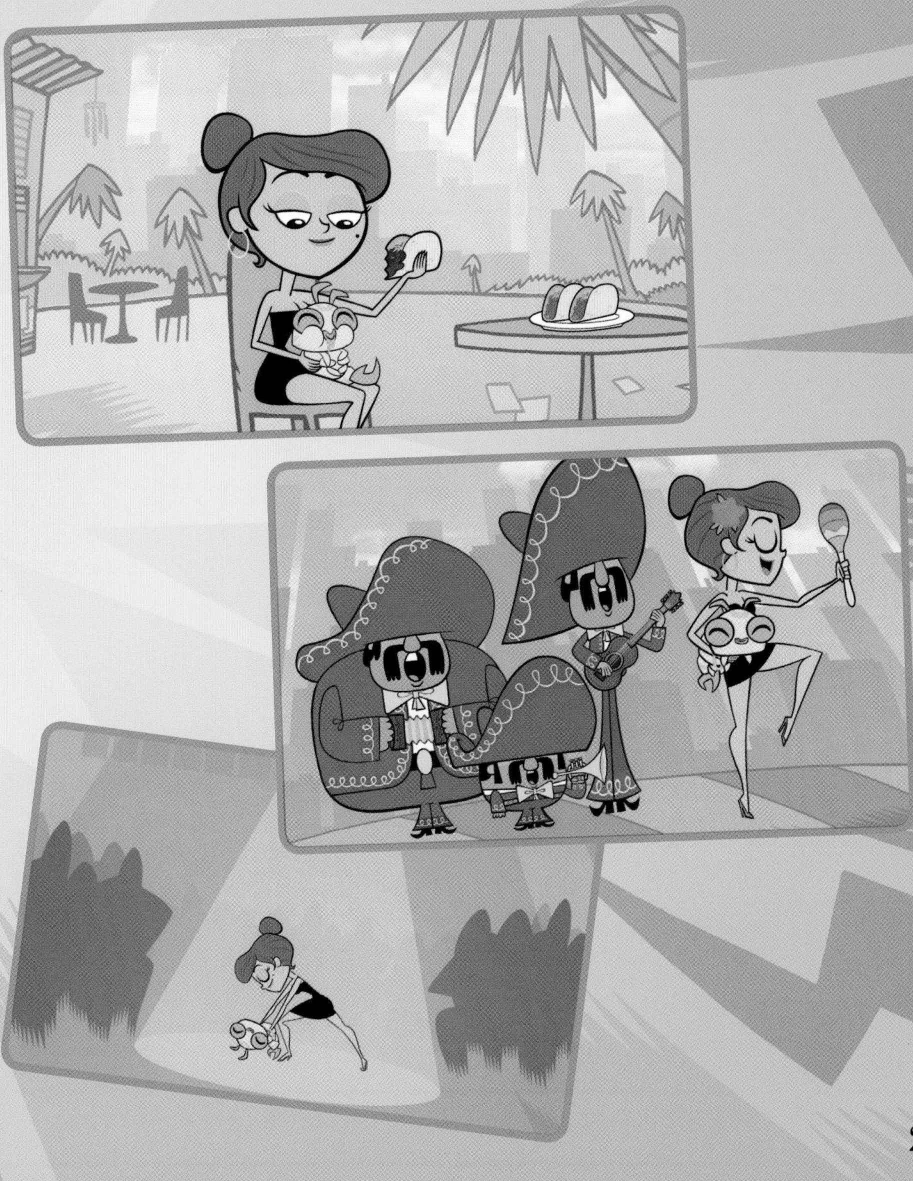

Sophia has a mean friend
named Carlos.
He locks up Sophia and Silkie!

Silkie is able to escape!

Carlos is so angry!
He challenges Silkie
to a sword fight.
Silkie wins!

When Silkie's adventures end,
he always returns home.

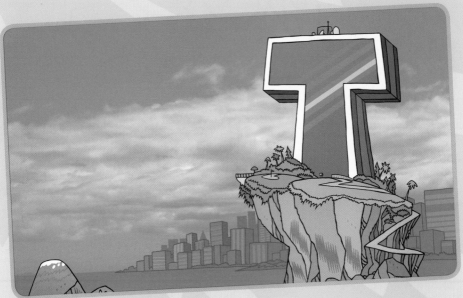

Starfire and the other Titans are so happy to see him!

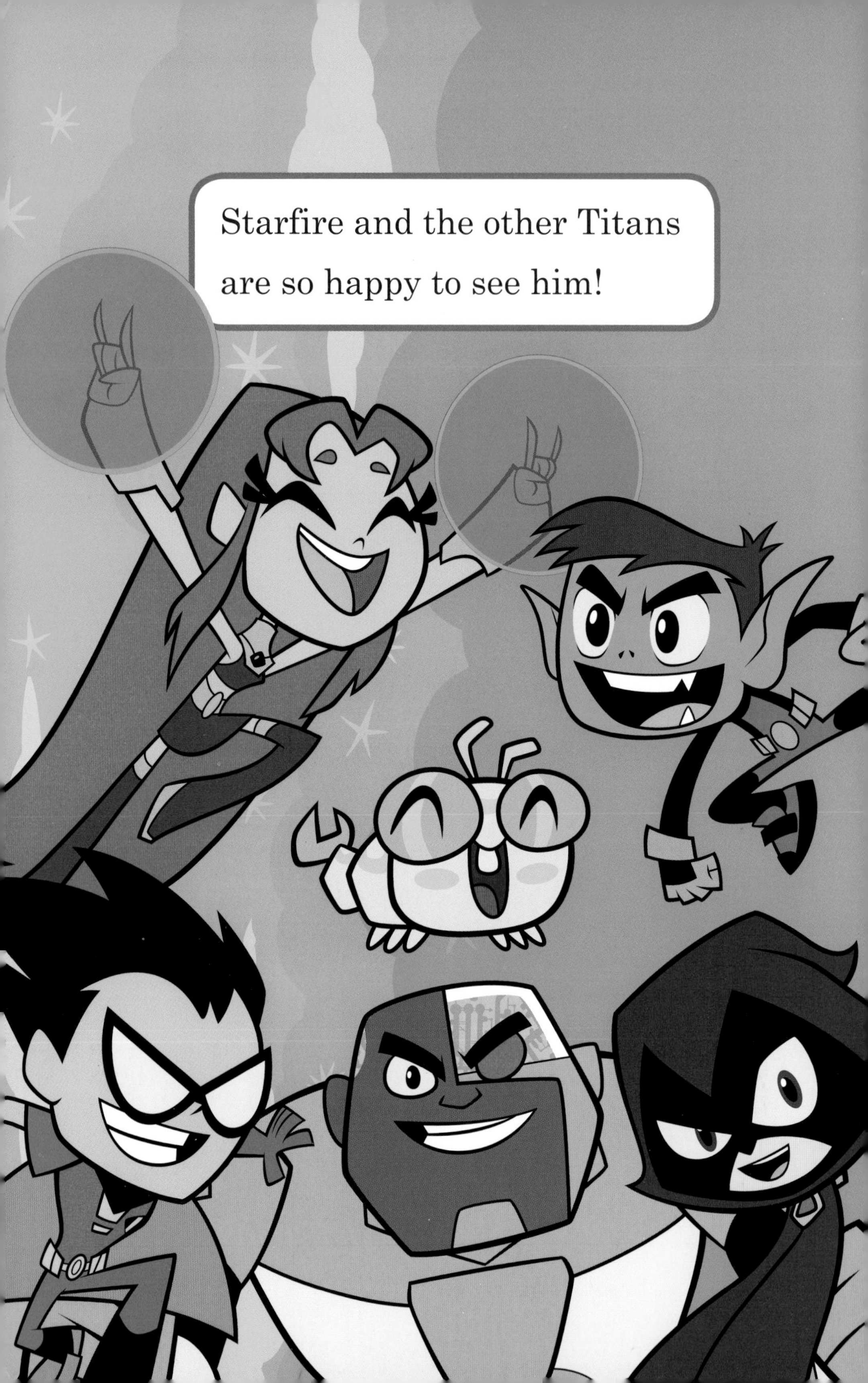